Puppy Mudge Wants to Play

Puppy Mudge
Wants to Play

By Cynthia Rylant

Illustrated by Suçie Stevenson

SCHOLASTIC INC.
New York   Toronto   London   Auckland   Sydney
Mexico City   New Delhi   Hong Kong   Buenos Aires

ISBN 0-439-77324-5

Text copyright © 2005 by Cynthia Rylant. Illustrations copyright © 2005 by Suçie Stevenson. All rights reserved. Published by Scholastic Inc., 557 Broadway, New York, NY 10012, by arrangement with Simon & Schuster Books for Young Readers, Simon & Schuster Children's Publishing Division. SCHOLASTIC and associated logos are trademarks and/or registered trademarks of Scholastic Inc.

12 11 10 9 8 7 6 5 4 3 2 1   6 7 8 9 10 11/0

Printed in the U.S.A.   23

First Scholastic printing, September 2006

READY-TO-READ is a registered trademark of Simon & Schuster, Inc.

Book design by Daniel Roode

The text for this book is set in Goudy.

The illustrations for this book are rendered in pen-and-ink and watercolor.

This is Henry's puppy, Mudge.
Mudge wants to play.

Henry is reading.
Henry does not want to play.

Mudge cannot read.

Mudge wants to play.

Mudge pulls off Henry's sock.

"Aw, Mudge," says Henry.

Henry reads.

Mudge chews up Henry's laces.

"Aw, Mudge," says Henry.

Henry reads.
Mudge sits on Henry's foot.

Mudge sits on Henry's lap.

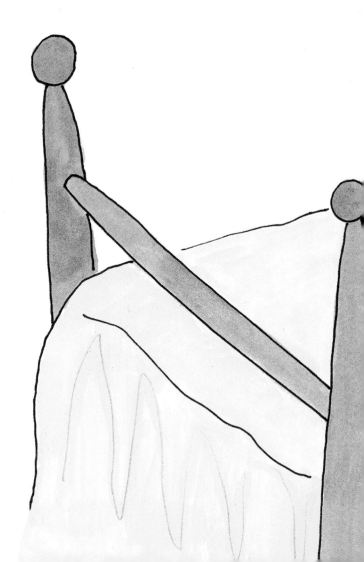

Mudge sits on Henry's book.
Mudge looks at Henry.

Mudge looks and looks and
looks at Henry.
"Mudge," asks Henry, "do you
want to play?"

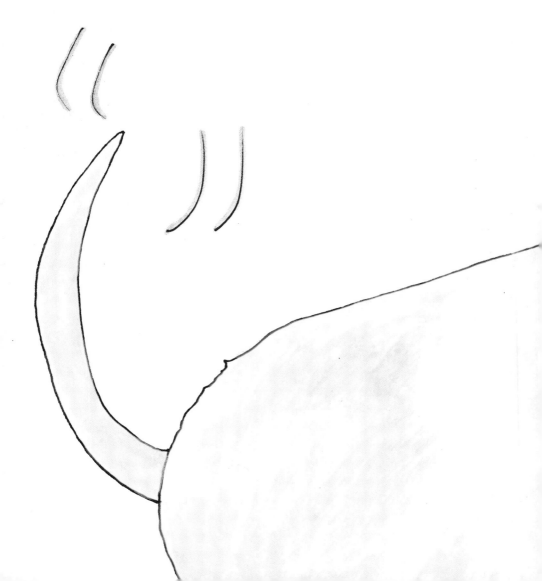

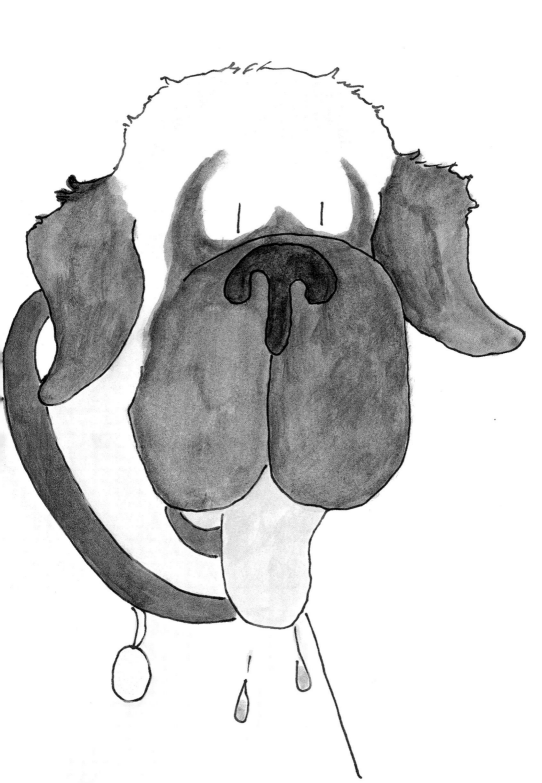

Mudge jumps.
Mudge dances.

Mudge goes round and round.

Mudge WANTS TO PLAY.

So they do!